NEW HAVEN PUBLIC
NEW HAVEN PUBLIC LIBRARY
3 5000 09492 5913

BO RABBIT SMART FOR TRUE

Folktales from the Gullah

BO RABBIT SMART FOR TRUE

Folktales from the Gullah

Retold by Priscilla Jaquith
Drawings by Ed Young

Philomel Books New York

Published by Philomel Books
a division of
The Putnam Publishing Group
200 Madison Avenue
New York, New York 10016

Library of Congress Cataloging in Publication Data

Jaquith, Priscilla.
Bo Rabbit smart for true.

These tales are based on tales recorded in 1949 for the Library of Congress which in 1955 issued a phonodisc under title: Animal tales told in the Gullah dialect by Albert H. Stoddard of Savannah, Georgia, edited by D. B. M. Emrich.

CONTENTS: Bo Rabbit smart for true.—Alligator's Sunday suit.—Bo Rabbit's hide-and-seek.—Rattlesnake's word.
1. Afro-American tales—Georgia. [1. Folklore, Afro-American. 2. Folklore—United States. 3. Cartoons and comics] I. Young, Ed. II. Emrich, Duncan, 1908- comp. Animal tales told in the Gullah dialect by Albert H. Stoddard of Savannah, Georgia. III. Stoddard, Albert Henry, 1872-1954. IV. Title.
PZ8.1.J35Bo 398.2′452′08996073 80-13275
ISBN 0-399-20793-7
ISBN 0-399-61179-7 lib. bdg.

Contents

For my grandchildren, Lisa and Susan Patton

Author's Foreword

Fringing the coasts of Georgia and South Carolina with their many Sea Islands is the land of the Gullah, a people brought to America by slave traders in the 1700s to work the rice and cotton fields of the plantation owners.

Nobody knows exactly where they came from. Some scholars, like Ambrose E. Gonzales, author of the "Black Border" books, trace them to Angola in West Africa. An entry of the Charleston City Council in 1822, referring to "Gullah Jack" and his company of "Gullah or Angola Negroes" seems to support this view. But there are others, like John Bennett, a long-time student of Gullah history, who believe they came from a tribe in Liberia known as the Golas whose quick, clipped speech at one time led them to be called "Quaquas" by the Dutch because their language reminded them of the gabbling of geese.

Whatever their exact origin, the Gullahs came either directly from Africa or via the Bahamas and West Indies and settled down on the southern coastal plantations. Isolated from the hinterland by pine barrens and tidal swamps, they developed their own customs, folklore and language. Some Gullahs—about 250,000 of them—still live there today in remote rural areas although cars, radio and TV have cut through their isolation and threatened their language with extinction.

Describing them after the Civil War, Reed Smith wrote in a bulletin of the University of South Carolina: "Amid the wreckage of great plantations, in the broomsedge fields, the lonely rice marshes, the windy pine woods, the dying rice fields, on the little truck farms and cotton patches of the lowlands, they remained, eking out an existence as best they could, almost as untouched by civilization as if they had still been dwelling in the forests of equatorial Africa."

Having settled in one of the greatest bird and game lands

in the United States, the Gullah hunted and fished until they knew every quirk and habit of the alligator, deer, fox, rabbit, partridge and other creatures that lived there. At night, around their cabin fires, they told tales about the wildlife of the woods and marshes, incorporating characters from their new environment into stories recalled from their African homeland.

The Gullah speak with a lilt a little like that of Calypso. Their language blends words from their native Africa (like "cooter" for tortoise from the African "kuta") with Elizabethan English and bits of dialect from Dorset, Devon or other British provinces (like the Suffolk word "bittles" for victuals). Many scholars have studied Gullah. Some, like Guy B. Johnson, think it can be traced back to English dialects spoken by indentured whites working with the Gullahs. Others, like Lorenzo Dow Turner, believe it stems directly from African languages such as Ewe, Fante, Wolof and Yoruba.

Whatever its source, the Gullah language is incomprehensible to the uninitiated. If someone said to you, "Oonah konnou oonah?" would you understand what that person was saying? That is part of the verbatim testimony given by a Gullah in a lawsuit following a collision between two sailboats and reported by Mr. Bennett. It means, "Whose boat is that?"

Gullah has its own vocabulary; it takes every possible shortcut, and it uses its own syntax and grammar. The same noun can be both singular and plural; the same verb, both past and present. For example: "E" is used for "he," "she" and "it." "Shum" is a shortcut for "see" or "saw," "him," "her," "it" or "them." So from two words, "E shum," you can get twenty-four possible sentences—you choose the most likely from the context.

In addition, words can have meanings quite foreign to standard English. When Crane tries to sip soup from a flat saucer with his long bill, the Gullah say his mouth can't "specify," meaning it doesn't work. And as a swift query, somewhat like the French "N'est-ce pas?", the Gullah sprinkle their talk with "enty?"

Many people have tried to write down this strange language. One of these was Albert H. Stoddard, who was born in

1872 on Daufuskie Island off South Carolina's coast and raised among the Gullah. On his return to the island from college, he began to set down their tales in dialect. Years later when he was seventy-seven, he recorded them exactly as he had heard them in his youth for the Archive of Folk Song of the Library of Congress. If you play his records and follow them with his transcriptions, you can begin to understand the language—not the "gabbling of geese" at all, but haunting, nimble poetry.

The tales in this book are based on Stoddard's work. Because Gullah is so difficult to understand, the language is not reproduced exactly; but in these stories an effort has been made to capture its flavor and lively humor. A bibliography has been included for those who wish to read more about the Gullah and their folklore.

—Priscilla Jaquith

Bo Rabbit Smart for True

One morning at first-day, Elephant was just lying down in his bed on the high hill when...

"Wait, Elephant! Wait!" cries a voice under his right leg.

Elephant holds his leg heist in the air. "Who's that?"

"It's me." Bo Rabbit hops out. "Why don't you watch what you do, Elephant? You almost mash me."

"You're too little," grumbles Elephant. "Nobody can see you."

"Little! I'm not too little. You're too big. You're one big man, Elephant." He watches Elephant stretch out in his bed. "You're even more big lying down than standing up."

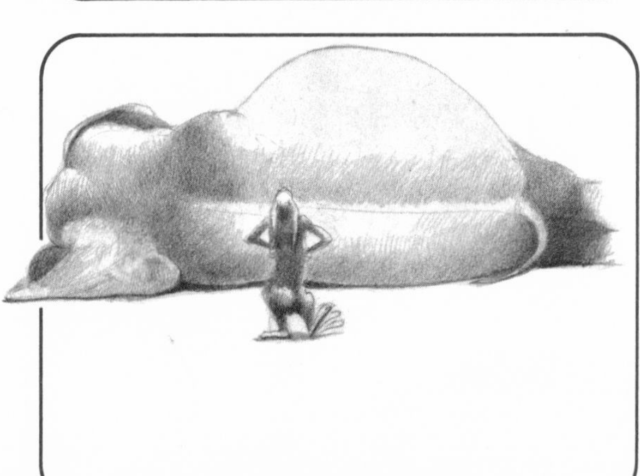

"I know. I'm the biggest thing on earth, Bo Rabbit."

"Elephant, you know one thing? If I wanted to, big as you are and little as I am, I could pull you right out your bed."

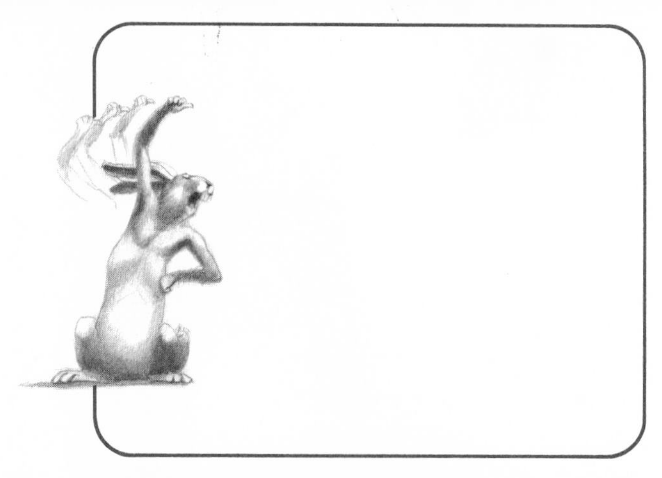

"What kind of talk you talking, Rabbit? I'm up all night. I come here for catch some sleep and you have to come botheration me about pull me out my bed. Go 'long and let me sleep."

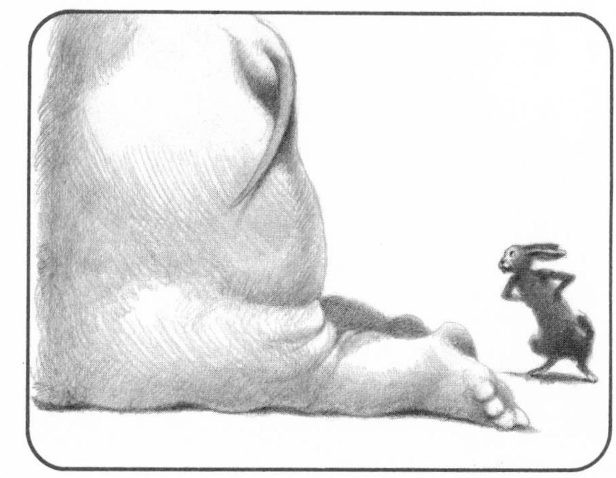

"Elephant, if I'm nigh you so your bigness scares me, I can't do it, for true. But if you let me tie one rope to you and get back in the brush where I can't see you, I bet I can pull you right out your bed."

"You couldn't move one of my ears, Rabbit."

"But if I do, Elephant, if I do, you never say I'm too little then, isn't it so?"

"All right, all right. Go away now."

Bo Rabbit takes his departure. He walks on and walks on, *kapot*, *kapot*, *kapot*, through the brush and down the hill till he reaches the ocean shore.

Far out in the blue, he sees Whale swimming.

"Hi there, Whale," he hollers.

Whale spouts, *Szi*, *Szi*, *Szi*, and leaps high to look towards shore. Then he swims close and pulls up with a great swish of his tail, SPASHOW.

"G'morning, Bo Rabbit."

"Where you been, Whale? I ain't seen you in a long time."

"I been clean around the earth, Rabbit."

"Gracious, Whale, you sure do grow to be one big man."

"I know. I'm the biggest thing in the water, Rabbit."

"Whale, you know one thing?"

"What, Bo Rabbit?"

"Little as I am and big as you are, if I wanted to, I could pull you right out the Salt."

Whale laughs till he splutters, *Shuplu, shuplu, shuplu*. "What kind of talk you talking, Rabbit? You couldn't *move* me in the ocean, let alone pull me out. You're too little."

"Oh, no, I'm not. If I'm there when you come out the water so your bigness scares me, I can't do it, for true. But if you let me tie one rope to you so I can go back on the hill where I can't see you, I bet I can pull you right out the sea. You never call me too little then, isn't it so?"

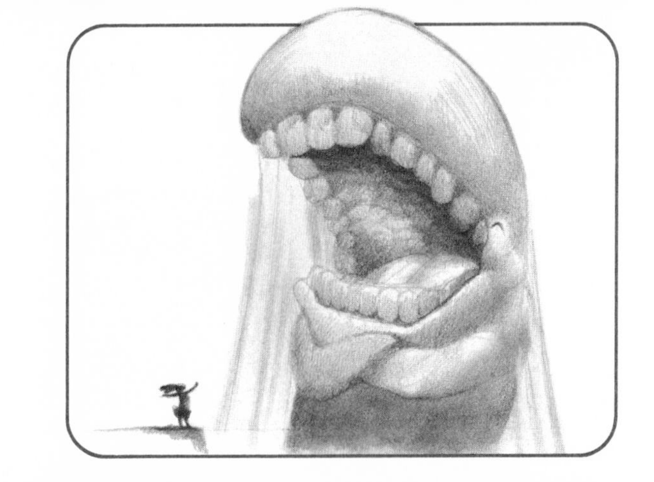

"All right, all right. I like to see that, Rabbit. I surely would."

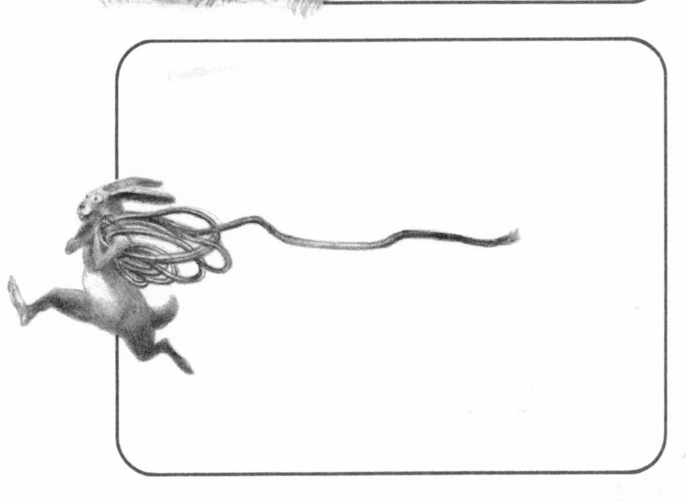

Bo Rabbit goes home and gets a long rope.

Then he takes his foot in his hand and runs to Elephant's house.

Elephant is in his bed asleep. Bo Rabbit yells, "Roll over, Elephant. Roll over."

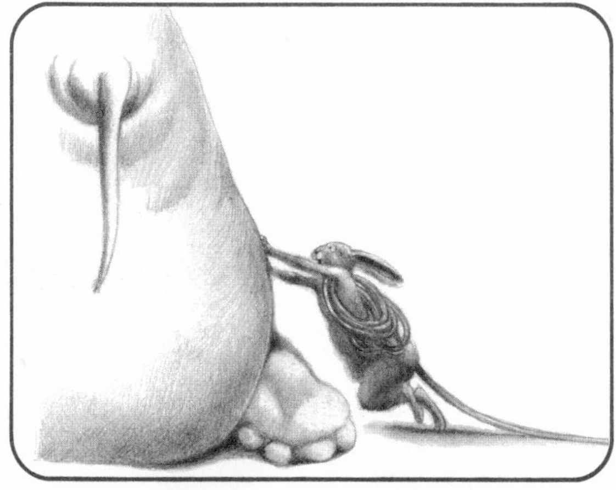

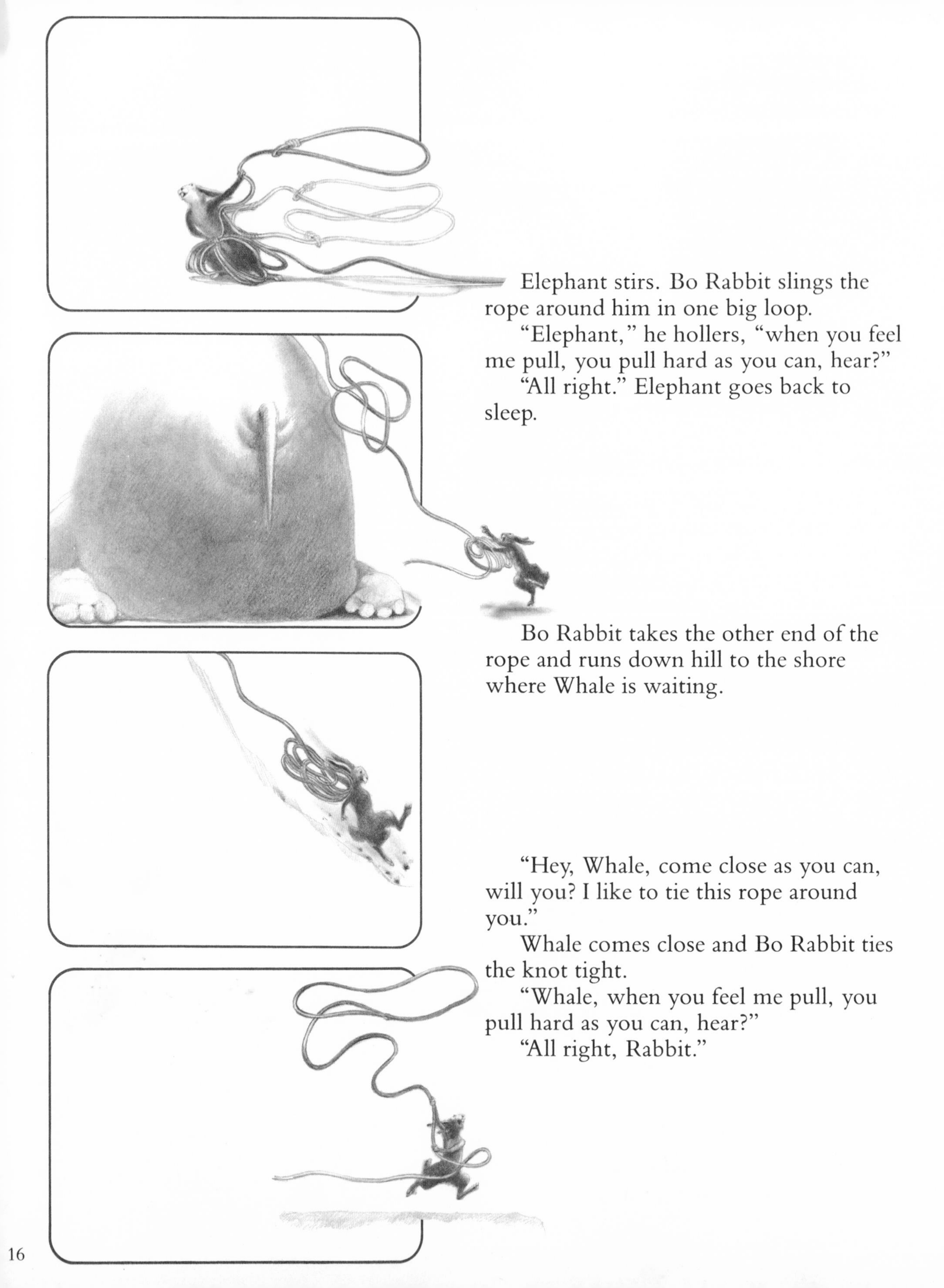

Elephant stirs. Bo Rabbit slings the rope around him in one big loop.

"Elephant," he hollers, "when you feel me pull, you pull hard as you can, hear?"

"All right." Elephant goes back to sleep.

Bo Rabbit takes the other end of the rope and runs down hill to the shore where Whale is waiting.

"Hey, Whale, come close as you can, will you? I like to tie this rope around you."

Whale comes close and Bo Rabbit ties the knot tight.

"Whale, when you feel me pull, you pull hard as you can, hear?"

"All right, Rabbit."

Bo Rabbit goes in the middle of the rope and he takes it in all two his hands and he pulls from all two ends one time, *hrup*, *hrup*, *hrup*.

Elephant, asleep in his bed, doesn't have Bo Rabbit in the back part of his head, but Whale is waiting in the water for see what Bo Rabbit will do.

When he feels Bo Rabbit make his pull, he gives a big jerk, KPUT.

The first thing Elephant knows, he's jerked out his bed and goes sumbleset down the hill, *Fahlip, fahlip, fahlip*.

He can't get on his foot. When he does, he starts to pull, *hrup, hrup, hrup*. But all he can pull, he keeps going to the sea.

Except he see two trees and brace himself against them, Whale would have pulled him clean into the sea and drowned him.

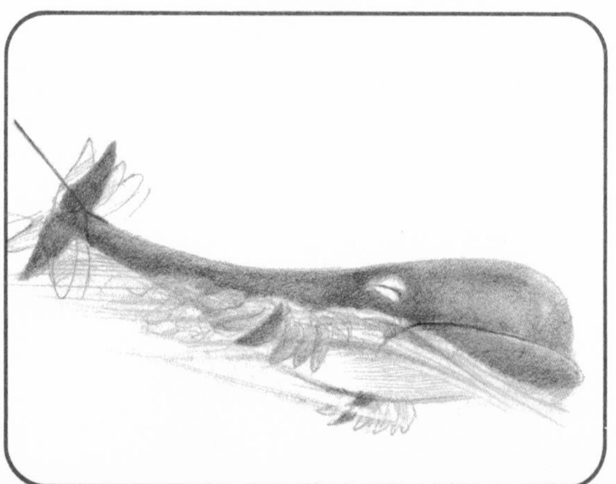

But all Whale pull, *hrup, hrup, hrup*, he can't pull Elephant out of those trees.

By and by in the sun-hot, Whale gets tired. He gives slack back on the rope and

Elephant takes that slack up the hill and pulls Whale clean out of the deep.

Except Whale hold onto a rock in the Salt, Elephant would have pulled him all the way to the high hill. But hard as Elephant pull, *hrup*, *hrup, hrup*, he can't pull Whale out of the sea.

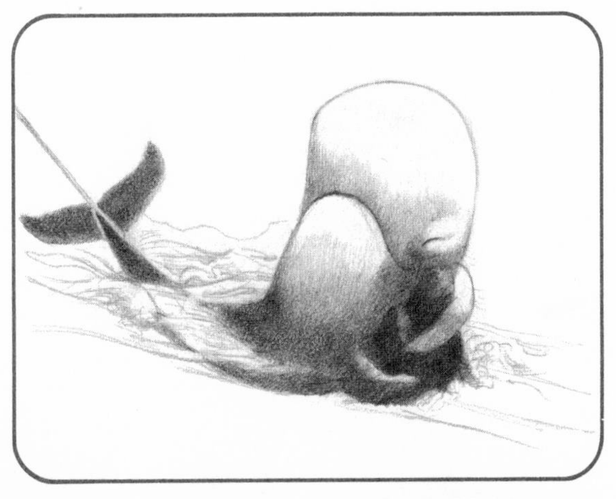

By and by in the sun-hot, Elephant gets tired. He gives back slack. Whale gives a jerk, KPUT, and pulls till he's back in the deep.

Bo Rabbit chuckles and takes out his pocket knife.

Directly Whale gets tired and Elephant goes back on the hill, Bo Rabbit slips out and cuts the rope in the middle, *sazip, sazip, sazip.*

Then he grabs the end of the rope tied to Elephant and runs after him.

"What you say now, Elephant?" he cries, dancing around him and waving the rope in the air. "What you say now? You're not in your bed, are you? I pulled you right out of it, didn't I? Didn't I?"

Elephant looks at the rope in Bo Rabbit's hand. "How do you do it, Bo Rabbit? Little as you are and big as I am, how do you do it?"

"I'm one able little man, Elephant. But I'm not too little, am I? Say I'm not too little or I jerk you right over my head and throw you in the sea and drown you for true."

"You're not too little," Elephant is hasty to say.

"All right. You can go now."

"So long, Bo Rabbit. Maybe I get some sleep at last." Elephant lumbers off to bed.

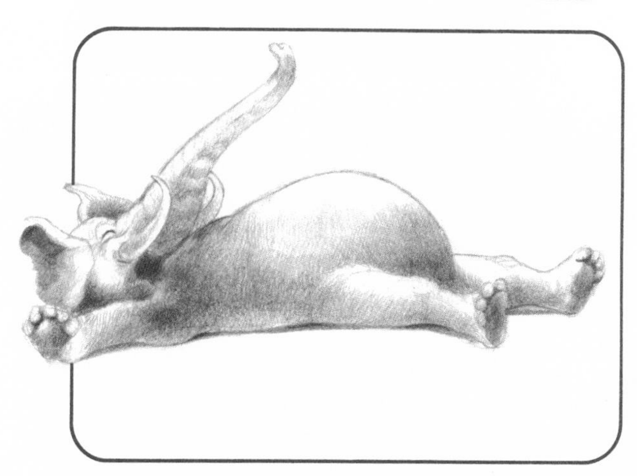

Bo Rabbit runs down hill and picks up the end of the rope tied to Whale. Then he goes to the shore where Whale is waiting.

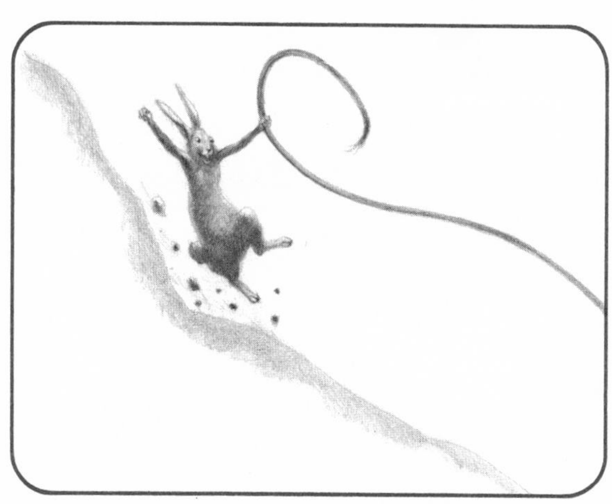

"What you say now, Whale?" he cries, dancing up and down and waving the rope in the air. "I pulled you clean out the deep, didn't I? Didn't I?"

Whale spouts, *Szi, szi, szi,* and looks at the rope in Bo Rabbit's hand. "How do you do it, Bo Rabbit? Little as you are and big as I am, how do you do it?"

"I'm one able little man, Whale. But I'm not too little, am I? Say I'm not too little or I jerk you right over my head and throw you up on the high hill."

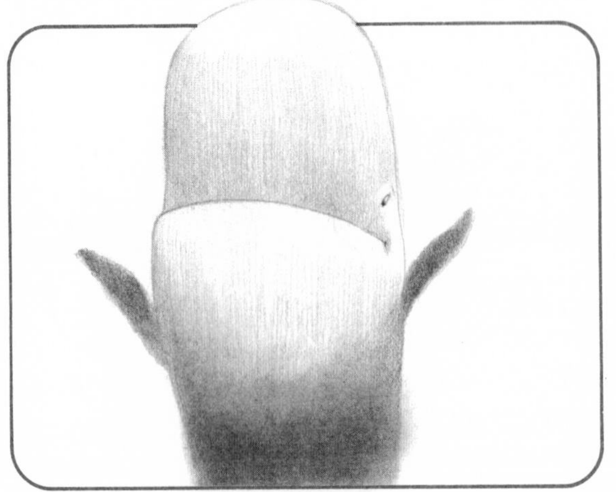

"You're not too little, Rabbit." Whale slaps the sea with his tail for emphasis, SPASHOW. "If you're any bigger, you can move the earth and flood the world and nobody be safe. Oh, no, you're not too little, Bo Rabbit. Not too little, at all."

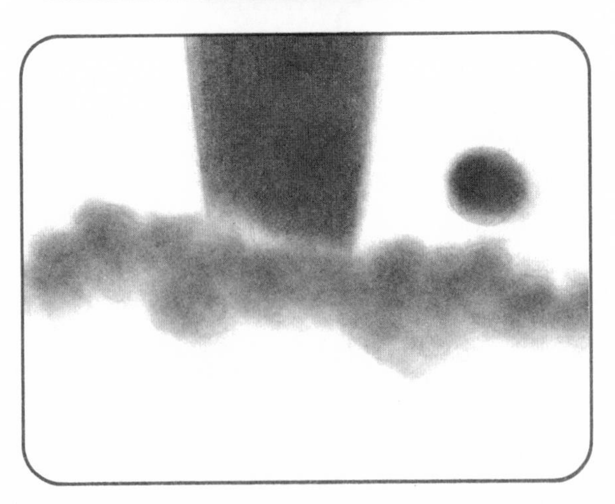

No matter how little you are, if you're smart for true, you can best the biggest crittuh in the sea and the biggest crittuh on earth. It stands so.

Alligator's Sunday Suit

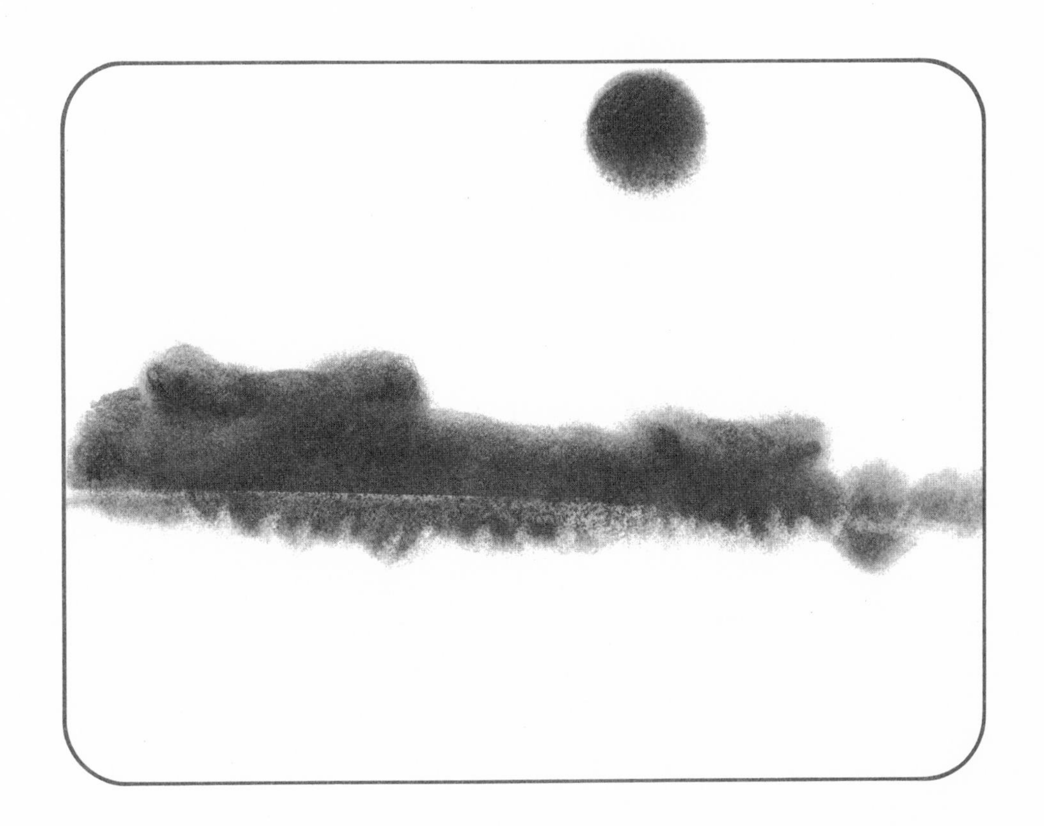

One day long ago, Alligator was floating in his home creek thinking how satisfy life is.

In those days, he's dress-up in a white suit good enough for Sunday all the time. He lives in the water with all the fish he can eat so he never has to work for a living. And he never, never meets up with trouble.

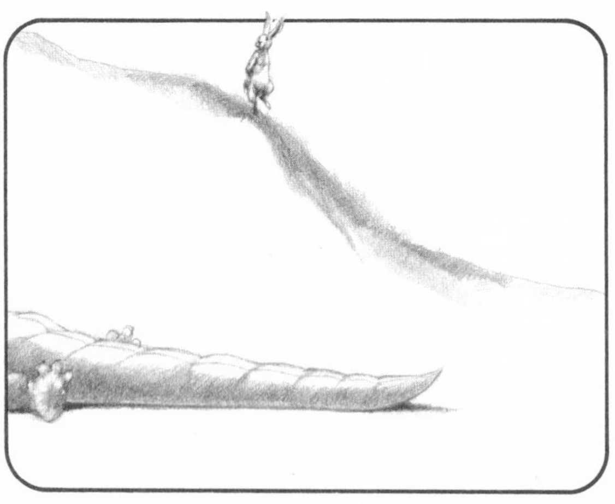

Well, Alligator is lazy in the sun-hot when here comes Bo Rabbit projecting along the creek shore.

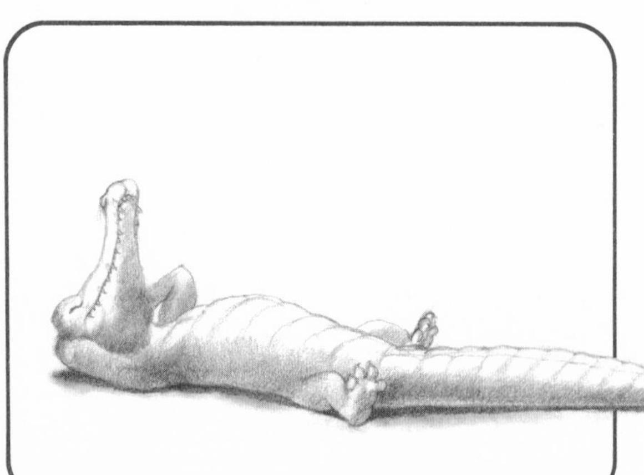

"G'morning, Alligator. How're you today?" asks Bo Rabbit, stopping to pass the time of day and other sociabilities.

"Doing just fine, thank you kindly. How's everyone to your house?"

"Oh, we making out. But so much trouble, Alligator. So much trouble."

"Trouble? What's that, Rabbit? I ain't never seen trouble."

"You ain't never seen trouble? Great Peace! I can show you trouble, Alligator."

"I'd like that, Bo Rabbit. I'd surely like to see how trouble stands."

"All right," Bo Rabbit makes response. "Meet me in the broomsage field tomorrow morning time the sun dries the dew off the grass good and I'll show you trouble."

Next morning time the sun gets high,

Alligator takes his hat and starts to leave the house. Miz Alligator asks him where he's going.

"I'm going to meet Bo Rabbit so he can show me how trouble stands."

"Well, if you're going to see trouble, I'm going, too."

"Hush up, you ain't going nowhere," says Alligator, high and mighty. "You best let me go see how trouble stands first. Then I can show you."

This makes Miz Alligator so mad she starts to arguefy.

They quarrel so loud till all the little alligators hear them and come sliding into the room, *hirr, hirr, hirr, hirr, hirr, hirr.*

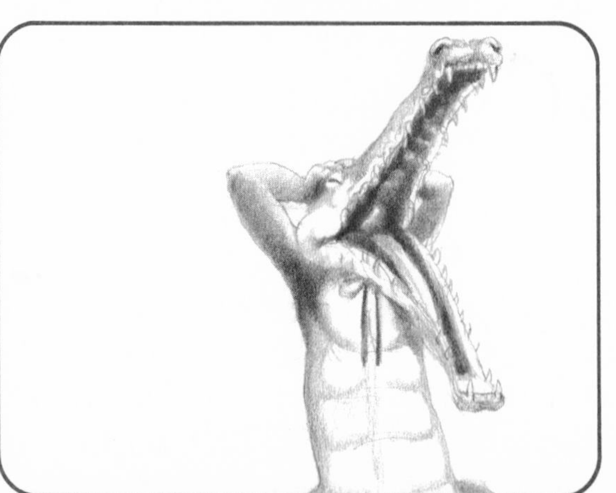

All the little alligators holler, "If you're going to see trouble, we're going, too. If you're going, we're going, too."

They make such a racket that to save his ears, Alligator roars, "Quiet! All right, all right. You *all* can come."

They cross the marsh and time they get in the broomsage field there's Bo Rabbit sitting on top a stump waiting for them.

"G'morning, Bo Rabbit," they say. And all the little alligators make their curtseys, *sazip*, *sazip*, *sazip*, *sazip*, *sazip*, *sazip*.

Bo Rabbit tells them "G'morning" back. "You all come to see trouble this morning, isn't it so?"

"It's so," says Alligator.

"It's so," say all the little alligators.

"All right. Stand out in the middle of the field and wait. I'll go get trouble and bring it."

Alligator, Miz Alligator and all the little alligators slither into the field, KAPUK, *Kapuk*, *kapuk*, *kapuk*, *kapuk*, *kapuk*, *kapuk*, *kapuk*.

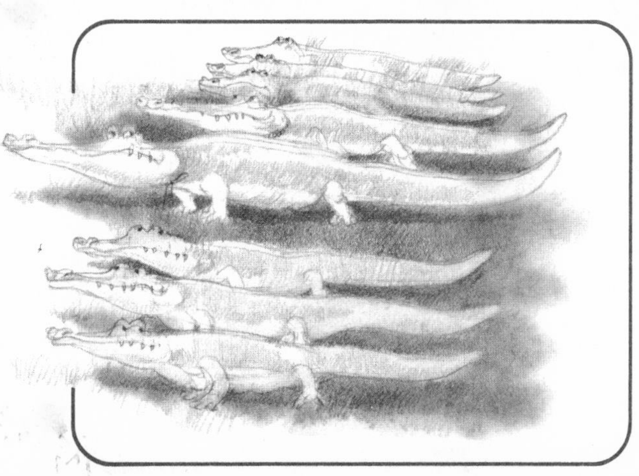

Bo Rabbit runs to the far edge and cuts him a hand of broomsage. Then he puts fire to it and runs it round and round the field till the fire runs round and round the field.

Miz Alligator sees the fire jumping up red and the smoke rising. "What's that yonder, Alligator?" She lives in the river and the wet marsh and never sees fire.

Alligator runs his eye around and shakes his head in puzzlement.

"I think that's the trouble Rabbit is bringing to show us," says Miz Alligator.

All the little alligators jump up and down and holler, "Ain't trouble pretty, Ma? Ain't trouble pretty?"

Soon the fire hot gets close and the smoke gets bad and all the alligators take out for one side of the field. They meet the fire.

They turn around to the other side. They meet the fire.

The fire gets so close it feels like it's going to burn them.

They all shut their eye and throw their head close to the ground and bust through the fire and never stop till, SPASHOW, Alligator jumps in the creek.

Right behind him, *Spashow*, Miz Alligator jumps in the creek.

Then all the little alligators come, *shu*, *shu*, *shu*, *shu*, *shu*, *shu*, in the creek.

As they scramble out, Bo Rabbit yells across the stream, “You’ve seen trouble now, Alligator. You like to see it again? I can show you.”

“No, suh, Bo Rabbit. No, suh,” says Alligator.

He looks at his suit. His white suit good enough for Sunday is gone.

He is blackish-green and rough and bumpy just the way he stands till yet.

"It's all Bo Rabbit's fault. Him and his Judas ways," says Alligator.

But even as the words come out his mouth, Alligator knows in his spirit that's not rightly so. He's the one asked to see trouble.

"I've learned one lesson for all my life," says Alligator. "Don't go looking for trouble, else you might find it."

Bo Rabbit's Hide-and-Seek

One evening at sun-cool Bo Rabbit was pleasuring himself in the meadow

when he sees Eagle's speck in the sky

grow big as a sandfly and then big as a sparrow.

Before Eagle can fall on him,

SWOOSH,

Bo Rabbit takes his foot in his hand and runs till he tumbles into the bramble patch.

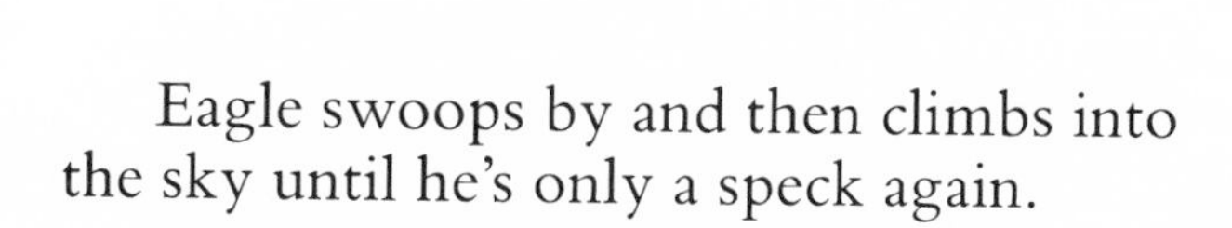

Eagle swoops by and then climbs into the sky until he's only a speck again.

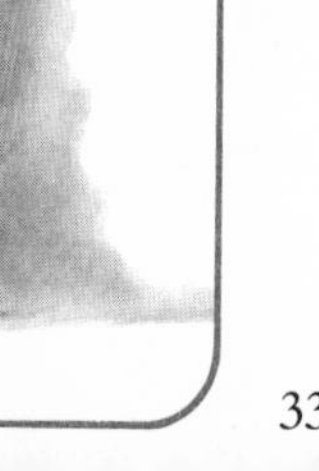

"That was close, Rabbit," says a voice from the clearing nearby.

Bo Rabbit looks. He can't see anyone. Then Partridge steps out, KIPIT.

Behind him comes Miz Partridge, *Kipit.* And behind her, all the little partridges, *kipit, kipit, kipit ...*

"Evening, Miz Partridge. Been a long time, Partridge, since I see you," says Bo Rabbit. "Long enough for you to start a family, I see.

And a mighty handsome family, too. Mighty handsome."

"Thank you kindly, Rabbit." Partridge stops abruptly, PIDUK. Miz Partridge stops fast, *Piduk,* and all the little partridges stop, bumping into each other, *piduk, piduk, piduk ...*

Partridge looks fondly at them. "Such a handful. So unmannersable." He shakes his head. "So hard to bring young ones up right today, Rabbit, isn't it so?"

Miz Partridge nods agreement and Bo Rabbit scratches his head. "What kind of bringing up you have in mind, Partridge? You mean how to act or when to act? Like when Eagle swoops, you run fast?"

"Run?" Partridge was shocked. "Hide is the way to fool Eagle. Why, before these children can fly, Rabbit, they learn to hide."

"You're wrong to teach 'hide,' Partridge. 'Run' is what to teach," says Bo Rabbit. "Anyone can hide. Why, I can hide better than anyone in the world."

"*Tsip*," chirps Miz Partridge in astonishment and "*tsip, tsip, tsip,*" cheep all the little partridges.

"Better than Dad?" says the littlest.

Partridge frowns at him. "Of course not. Rabbit knows nobody hides better than me."

"I surely don't know that, Partridge. I surely don't. Why, if I was to try, I could hide so nobody could find me."

"Go along, Rabbit. You always got so much to say for yourself."

"Show him, Dad. Show him you can hide better," cry all the little partridges hopping up and down, *ki, ki, ki* . . .

"I'll prove it to you, Partridge. Any time, any place you say."

"All right, Rabbit. Meet me in the clearing by the big log tomorrow at sun-up and I'll show you how to hide."

Next morning Bo Rabbit goes to the clearing. Partridge and his family are sitting on a log, waiting.

"Morning, Rabbit," says Partridge. "Here's the way for us to do.

First you hide yourself and when you hide good, you *whoop.* When I hear you *whoop*, I'll go hunt you. Then it's my turn to hide."

"All right," says Bo Rabbit.

He goes into the brush and hides himself underneath a bush where nobody can see him. Then he *whoops.*

Now when Bo Rabbit hides, he's so scared someone will come up on top of him and catch him and he won't see them coming that he keeps running his eye out of the bush so he can look all around.

When Partridge hears Bo Rabbit *whoop,* he starts hunting.

Miz Partridge stays comfortable on the log where she can keep an eye on the children. They are very mannersable and stay quiet, just watching.

Partridge looks this way and that. Right away, he sees Bo Rabbit's big eye shine out of the bush.

"I see you, Rabbit," he says. "Anybody could see you. Your big eye shine a mile."

"Good for you, Dad. Good, good," cry all the little partridges hopping up and down, *ki, ki, ki*...

Now it's Partridge's turn. He tells Bo Rabbit the very exact spot he's going to hide himself. Then he goes down to that exact spot and hides.

And then he *whoops.*

When Bo Rabbit hears him *whoop,* he starts hunting. All the little partridges follow and watch.

Bo Rabbit goes to that exact spot and he doesn't see Partridge. He looks all about and he doesn't see Partridge.

He takes his hand and parts all the grass, yet he doesn't see Partridge.

He gets down on his hands and knees and he turns all the leaves and he searches all about, all about for a long time. He still doesn't see Partridge.

By and by, Bo Rabbit gets tired. He stands up on his feet. "Partridge, I give up."

"If you do, then move from on top of me so I can get up," says Partridge.

Bo Rabbit jumps aside and Partridge rises.

Bo Rabbit looks at Partridge. He sees how his feather stands like the bark upon the tree and the dead leaf upon the ground. He knows now that when the hungry varmint hunts his dinner through the wood he can be right on top of Partridge and never know where he is.

“You’re right, Partridge,” he says. “You’re right to teach your children hide is best. You got the feather to hide. I got the long leg to run.”

Miz Partridge hops down from the log and all the little partridges start jumping up and down and cheeping, “You did it, Dad. You did it. You showed Rabbit how to hide.”

“Children, behave,” says Partridge. “There’s no call to jubilate. Rabbit knows now what’s right for some of us ain’t necessarily right for others.

We each got our own ways and we best accommodate ourselves and respect each other. Isn’t it so, Rabbit?”

“Yes, suh, Partridge,” says Bo Rabbit, “Yes, suh.”

Rattlesnake's Word

One windy day before sun-up Rattlesnake was slithering through the piney wood when BRAM a dead branch falls and pins him to the ground.

Rattlesnake is so vexed he sings his rattle, *Sssszzz, Sssszzz, Sssszzz.* Then he twists and coils to get out from under that branch. But twist and coil till he's tuckered out, he can't get free.

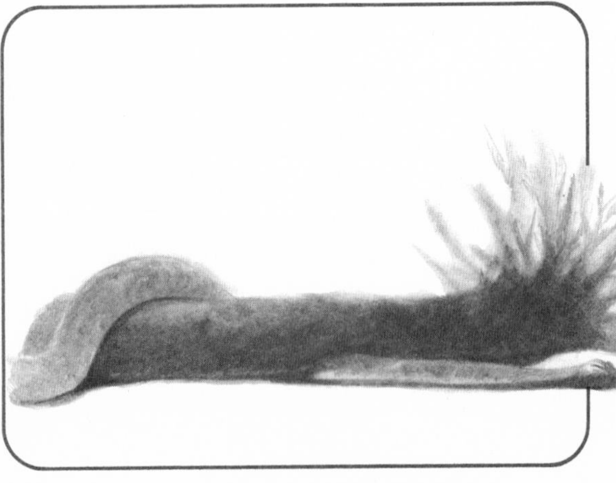

"I best wait till somebody comes by and lifts this log," he says to himself.

But nobody comes. Day-in-the-morning turns to day-clean. Still nobody comes.

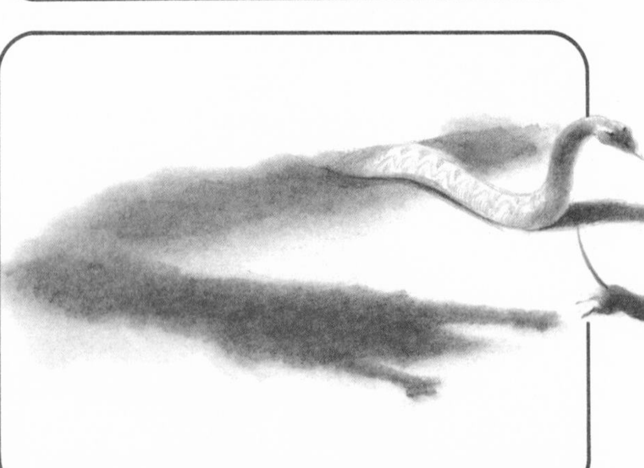

By and by, *skt, skt, skt,* a twig breaks. Rattlesnake turns his head.

Here comes Mouse running for his life and Fox after him.

Suddenly, *pufu, pufu, pufu,* Mouse pops down a hole and Fox pounces at air.

"Hi, Fox, I hope Mouse recognize his luck. You're the finest hunter in the wood, all the world knows that," says Rattlesnake, and he makes a great admiration over him. "You steal up and drop on a crittuh so quick he never knows it till he's dead. You tote a mighty heavy game bag there, Fox, mighty heavy."

Fox combs his flank with his tongue. "I been after dinner all night, Rattlesnake. Hungry won't catch me for a while. But how come you get under that log?"

"Accident, Fox, accident. I'm minding my own business when BRAM this branch falls on me. Come, move it off of me, do, Fox. My back is hurting bad."

"Why would I do that?" asks Fox. "Once I do that, you charm me with your eye till I move close and then you bite me dead."

"Would I do that to a friend who helps me?" asks Rattlesnake. "Oh, no, Fox, I never do that."

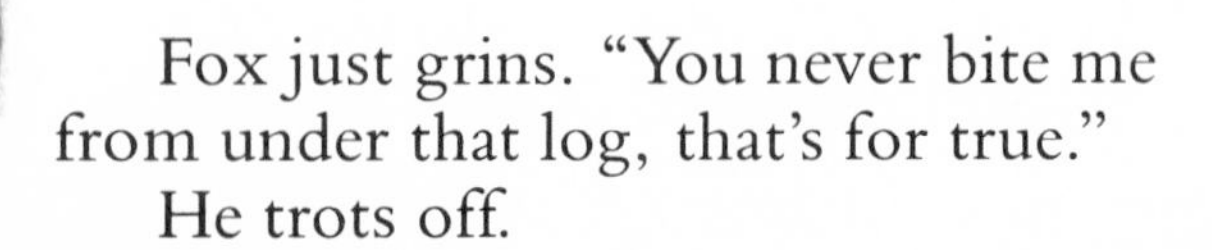

Fox just grins. "You never bite me from under that log, that's for true."

He trots off.

Rattlesnake composes himself. Nobody comes. Day-clean turns to middle-of-the-day and he gets hot. Still nobody comes.

By and by, *bbzzz, bbzzz, bbzzz,* a bee flies past. After it comes Bear, his eye fast to watch it and his foot to follow.

"Hi, Bear," calls Rattlesnake.

Bear pays him no mind. He keeps going till he reaches a dead tree. He starts to climb it.

Halfway up, Bear stops and sticks his arm into a hole. Then he pulls out his hand and licks it.

"Bear found him a wild honey tree," says Rattlesnake to himself. "When he comes by again, happy from all that sweetness, he sets me free for sure."

Presently here comes Bear again, easy and slow, his mouth all sticky.

"Hi, Bear," says Rattlesnake. "Mighty nice harvest you catch there. But all the crittuhs know you're the clever one to track down the wild bee and find the sweetest honey in the wood."

Bear licks his mouth. "It is sweet for true. But how come you get under that log, Rattlesnake?"

"Accident, Bear, accident. This branch blows down and BRAM it lands on top of me. Come move it off of me, Bear, do. My back is hurting bad."

"Why do I do that, Rattlesnake?" asks Bear. "If I do that, you charm me with your eye till I move close and then you bite me dead."

"Would I do that to a friend who helps me?" asks Rattlesnake. "Oh, no, Bear, I never do that."

"You promise?"

"I promise."

Bear lifts the log, *hrup, hrup, hrup.*

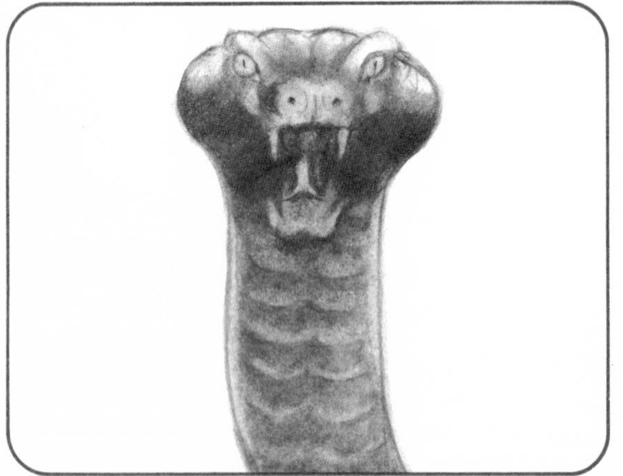

Before he can even turn his head, Rattlesnake fixes him with his cold eye and charms him till he can't move. Bear stands there all a-tremble and tries to hold himself from going closer and closer till he gets so close Rattlesnake can bite him dead.

Just then, *Scrr, Scrr, Scrr,* comes the scuffle of someone landing on a pile of dead leaves. Bear hears it and has just enough sense left to holler, "Help, whoever it is, help, help."

"It's me, Bo Rabbit. What's wrong, Bear?"

"Nothing's wrong, Rabbit," says Rattlesnake. "Me and Bear just having a friendly little get-together is all."

"That so, Bear?"

"No, Rabbit." Bear tells him the truth. "Now Rattlesnake charms me and I can't move."

Bo Rabbit hops over to the log and studies it. "You never been caught under there, Rattlesnake. I don't believe it."

"You're wrong, Rabbit. I surely was fasten under that log."

"How can you be? The one end of the log is heisted high on that rock. You got room for you and half your family under there."

Rattlesnake darts a look. "Oh, that's not where the log was, Rabbit. When Bear lifts it off of me, he throws it off a-ways."

"Rattlesnake, I never believe you caught under that log till I see with my own eyes where it was."

"You don't believe me? You calling me a liar?" Rattlesnake is getting vexed. "Bear, move that log back where it was."

Bear puts it back, *hrup, hrup, hrup.*

Bo Rabbit hops around and around it, quizzing it with his eyes. "It's flat to the ground, Rattlesnake. You never been under there. You're too fat to get under."

Rattlesnake is that vain about his figure, his long, slim figure, that he rises up in rage.

"Fat? Me too fat?" He sings his rattle, *Sssszzz, Sssszzz, Sssszzz.* "You call me fat, Rabbit. And you call me a liar. Bear, lift up that log. I show you, Rabbit."

Bear lifts the log, *hrup, hrup, hrup* and Rattlesnake slides under.

Bo Rabbit whispers, "Drop it, Bear, drop it!"

Bear drops the log and pins Rattlesnake to the ground once more. He sings his rattle again in fury, *Sssszzz, Sssszzz, Sssszzz.* Then he twists and coils to get out but he can't. He's caught tight.

"Thank you, Rabbit, thank you kindly," says Bear as they set off through the wood.

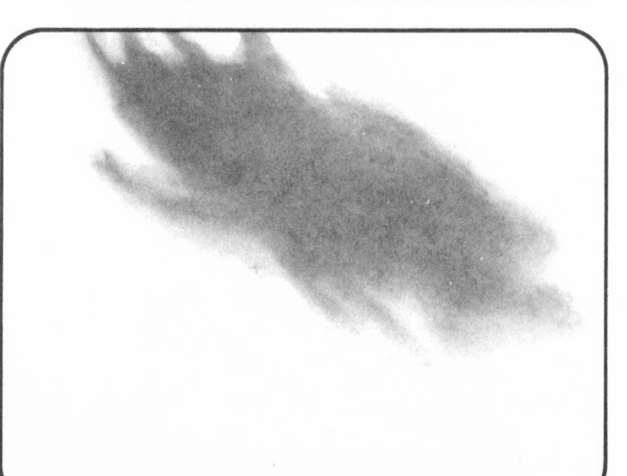

"Glad to oblige, Bear. Just goes to show you got to study who says a thing before you take it for true. A crittuh's word is only as good as the crittuh who gives it. It stands so."

Notes

Some of the Gullah tales, like most folktales, trace their roots to far countries and are centuries-old. Others seem to have originated long ago in the southern United States. Scholars think many reached Europe from India and were then carried to Africa by Portuguese, Spanish and Dutch sailors. From there, they were brought to the Americas, sometimes by Africans, sometimes by voyagers from Europe.

Bo Rabbit Smart For True: In 1893, Professor Adolph Gerber reported an almost exact duplication of this tale from the island of Mauritius in the Indian Ocean. Hare is the hero instead of Rabbit and he challenges Elephant and Whale and wins by tying them together. Herbert H. Smith reported a variant from Brazil in 1879 in which a tortoise insists he is stronger than a tapir and can pull him into the sea. When the tapir threatens to pull the tortoise into the wood and kill him, the tortoise gets a vine stem, ties one end to the tapir and the other to the tail of a whale. Then he goes into the forest and shakes the vine until both animals start pulling.

Alligator's Sunday Suit: Several versions of this tale have been reported from the South. In 1888, Charles C. Jones, Jr., in his *Negro Myths from the Georgia Coast* told how Rabbit, learning that Alligator had never seen trouble, waited until he fell asleep in the broomsage and then set it on fire around him. In 1892, Mrs. A. M. H. Christensen reported a version from the Sea Islands of South Carolina in which when Alligator asks to see trouble, Rabbit tells him to go to the broomsage field when the wind is blowing from the "Norderwest." Elsie Clews Parsons recorded in 1917 (*JAF*, 30: 179) a tale from Guilford County, North Carolina, about a terrapin in a brush-heap who volunteers to keep Rabbit company on a walk. When Rabbit finds Terrapin can't keep up, he sets the brush-heap on fire. "'I reckon you'll run now.' 'No, I'll crawl.' 'Then you'll do it mighty fast.'" Joel Chandler Harris told a version of "Alligator's Sunday Suit" in which Rabbit, running for his life from a dog, happens on Alligator. Because Alligator never meets trouble himself, he laughs at Rabbit's plight and then crawls into the broomsage for a nap, whereupon Rabbit fires the grass and introduces him to trouble.

Bo Rabbit's Hide-and-Seek: Elsie Clews Parson (*Memoirs of JAF*, 16: 1923) reports a variant of this story from Hilton Head, one of the Sea Islands off South Carolina. Partridge bets Rabbit he can hide in a patch of broomsage so well that Rabbit can't find him. Rabbit, sure he'll win the bet, agrees to give Partridge one of his children if he fails. Rabbit hunts and hunts. Then, convinced Partridge can't be there, Rabbit sets the grass on fire. Partridge, having won the bet, flies up, goes home, and takes a rabbit child.

It's interesting to note in connection with this tale that in 1893 Professor Adolph Gerber in tracing the origin of the Uncle Remus stories reported that he could find no instance in Old World folklore in which one animal gets another into trouble by burning grass.

Rattlesnake's Word: So widespread is this story that in "The Folk Tale," Stith Thompson called it "Type 155," "Ungrateful Serpent Returned to Captivity." Perhaps the oldest authenticated variant stems from tales about Reynard the Fox which circulated in the Middle Ages on the Flemish border, and were first written down in the Twelfth Century in Latin, German and, as the "Roman de Renard," in French. A Flemish version of parts of the "Roman de Renard," known as "Reynaert de Vos," includes the story of a man who rescues a snake from a snare when the snake promises not to injure him. Once the snake is released, it threatens him, however, and the man appeals to a raven, bear and wolf who all refuse to condemn the snake. Finally, the man seeks arbitration from the fox, who insists that both the man and the snake resume their original positions before judgment. Substitute Bo Rabbit for the fox and Bear for the man and you have a forerunner of this Gullah tale.

Even more similar to "Rattlesnake's Word" is this version from the Hottentots of South Africa reported by W. H. I. Bleek in 1864: a man rescues Snake from under a rock and is then himself rescued by Jackal who insists he won't believe Snake was under the rock unless he sees it with his own two eyes.

From Mexico comes a story reported by F. Boas in 1912 in the *Journal of American Folk-Lore* (*JAF*, 25) of a rabbit rescuing a serpent from under a stone and asking a horse, steer and donkey for help. After they all refuse, a rooster steps in to save the rabbit.

According to Herbert H. Smith, writing in 1879, Tupi Indians along the Amazon tell another variant in which a fox or opossum finds a jaguar stuck in a hole. Once released, the jaguar threatens to eat the fox. A wise man passing by saves the fox by tricking the jaguar into going back in the hole.

Bibliography

W. R. BASCOM: *Acculturation Among the Gullah Negroes, American Anthropologist*, 43: 43–50, 1941.

JOHN BENNETT: *Gullah, a Negro Patois, The South Atlantic Quarterly*, Oct. 1908, Part I, 332–347 and Part II, 39–52.

W. H. I. BLEEK: *Reynard, the Fox, in South Africa; or Hottentot Fables and Tales*, T. Rübner and Company, London, 1864.

F. BOAS: *Notes on Mexican Folklore, Journal of American Folk-Lore*, 25: 204–260, 1912.

STELLA BREWER BROOKES: *Joel Chandler Harris, Folklorist*, University of Georgia Press, 1950.

T. F. CRANE: Review of Cosquin's "Contes Populaires de Lorraine," *Modern Language Notes*, 2: 87–91, April, 1887.

MRS. A. M. H. CHRISTENSEN: *Afro-American Folk Lore Told Round Cabin Fires on the Sea Islands of South Carolina*, J. G. Cupples Co., Boston, 1892.

MASON CRUM: *Gullah: Negro Life in the Carolina Sea Islands*, Duke University Press, Durham, N. C., 1940.

DUNCAN EMRICH: *Folklore on the American Land*, Little, Brown, Boston, 1972.

WILLIAM J. FAULKNER: *The Days When the Animals Talked: Black American Folktales and How They Came to Be*, Follett Publishing Co., Chicago, 1977.

ADOLPH GERBER: *Uncle Remus Traced to the Old World, Journal of American Folk-Lore*, 6: 245–257, 1893.

AMBROSE E. GONZALES: *The Black Border; Gullah Stories of the Carolina Coast*, The State Co., Columbia, S. C., 1922.

____________________: *With Aesop Along the Black Border*, The State Co., Columbia, S. C., 1924.

____________________: *The Captain, Stories of the Black Border*, The State Co., Columbia, S. C., 1924.

____________________: *Laguerre, a Gascon of the Black Border*, The State Co., Columbia, S. C., 1924.

JOEL CHANDLER HARRIS: *Uncle Remus: His Songs and His Sayings*, Houghton Mifflin Co., Boston and New York, 1915.

___________________: *Nights with Uncle Remus*, Houghton Mifflin Co., Boston and New York, 1911.

CHARLES F. HARTT: *Amazonian Tortoise Myths*, William Scully, Rio de Janeiro, 1875.

GUY B. JOHNSON: *Folk Culture on St. Helena Island, South Carolina*, Folklore Associates, Inc., Hatboro, Pa., 1968 (a reprint of the 1930 edition published by the University of North Carolina Press).

CHARLES COLCOCK JONES, JR.: *Negro Myths from the Georgia Coast Told in the Vernacular*, Houghton Mifflin Co., Boston and New York, 1888.

ERNEST MARTIN: *Le Roman de Renart*, Strasbourg and Paris, 1882.

ELSIE CLEWS PARSONS: *Folk-Lore of the Sea Islands, South Carolina*, American Folk-Lore Society, Cambridge, Mass., 1923 (*Memoirs of the American Folk-Lore Society*, 16, 1923).

___________________: *Tales from Guilford County, North Carolina*, *Journal of American Folk-Lore*, 30: 179, 1917.

HERBERT H. SMITH: *Brazil: the Amazons and the Coast*, S. Low, Marston, Searle and Rivington, 1879.

REED SMITH: *Gullah*; *Dedicated to the Memory of Ambrose E. Gonzales*, University of South Carolina Bureau of Publications, Columbia, S. C., 1926 (*Bulletin of the University of South Carolina*, No. 190, November, 1927).

SADIE H. STEWART: *Seven Folk-tales from the Sea Islands*, South Carolina, *Journal of American Folk-Lore*, 32: 394–396, 1919.

ALBERT H. STODDARD: *Animal Tales Told in the Gullah Dialect*, Archive of Folk Song Recordings, Library of Congress, Washington, D.C., 1949.

STITH THOMPSON: *The Folktale*, The Dryden Press, New York, 1946.

LORENZO DOW TURNER: *Africanisms in the Gullah Dialect*, University of Chicago Press, Chicago, 1949.

F. M. WARREN: *Uncle Remus and the Roman de Renard*, *Modern Language Notes*, 4: 129–135, May, 1890.

MARCELLUS S. WHALEY: *The Old Types Pass; Gullah Sketches of the Carolina Sea Islands*, Christopher Publishing House, Boston, 1925.

ABOUT THE AUTHOR

Priscilla Jaquith has always been interested in folktales and when her own grandchildren became old enough to appreciate them too it seemed just the right time to write this book. The author of numerous articles which have appeared in many different publications, this is Ms. Jaquith's first book. She lives in Hastings-on-Hudson, New York, where in addition to writing she enjoys birdwatching and painting.

ABOUT THE ARTIST

Ed Young is the well-known illustrator of many distinguished books for children, among them THE EMPEROR AND THE KITE by Jane Yolen, which was an Honor Book for the Caldecott Award; THE ROOSTER'S HORNS: *A Chinese Puppet Play to Make and Perform*, by Ed Young with Hilary Beckett; THE TERRIBLE NUNG GWAMA: *A Chinese Folktale*, by Ed Young, adapted from the retelling by Leslie Bonnet; and HIGH ON A HILL: *A Book of Chinese Riddles* by Ed Young. A graduate of the Los Angeles Art Center, he has taught art at Yale University and at Pratt Institute of Art in Brooklyn, N.Y. Born in Shanghai, China, Mr. Young now lives in Hastings-on-Hudson, New York.

Jaquith
Bo Rabbit smart for true: folktales from the Gullah.